GOLDIE and the SEA

Story by JUDITH SALTMAN
Pictures by KIM La FAVE

A MEADOW MOUSE PAPERBACK

Groundwood/Douglas & McIntyre

TORONTO/VANCOUVER

Goldie was nine and always looking.

She gazed at the world as if she were a fisherman waiting to catch its marvels in a net.

"It's all slippery, the world," she said to Foss, her cat. Foss always listened carefully to Goldie's thoughts. "You've got to be quick and quiet to catch the world, Foss."

"Quick—yes! Quiet—no!" squawked Goldie's parrot, Jake. "The world's all thunder and bluster, like the sea. Being a former pirate, I should know."

Goldie, Foss and Jake lived together in a little hushed house. Its roof was as red as a fire truck, and its chimney was stout and strong. Foss often sat on the chimney pot, as still as still all morning, staring into the sky.

One morning—much like any other—Goldie
and Foss sat at the kitchen table eating their
breakfast of porridge. Goldie liked sugar in her
porridge. Foss preferred salt. Neither could abide
raisins or lumps.

Jake hated porridge. "Not fit for a bird," he
said. "Give me some peanuts or crackerjack!"

Goldie always finished her porridge right down
to the bottom of the bowl. It was decorated with

blue and white pictures of Chinese waterfalls and
tiny bent men with tangled beards and twisted
walking sticks, toiling their way up the hills. "Do
you think they might be going to the ocean, Foss?"
she asked.

After she had washed the bowls and spoons
and put them away, Goldie brought out her
coloured pencils and crayons and tried to draw the
sea.

Long ago, Goldie's grandfather lived by the
Baltic Sea. He had painted many pictures of that
sea, and had given one to Goldie for her very own.
She loved the way the dark waves broke from
corner to corner across the old canvas, and its
smell of dust and wind and turpentine and salt.

But Goldie had never seen a real sea. Even though she used all of her twenty-four coloured pencils to draw ragged, broken waves and rubbed her fat greasy crayons on the paper to make the frothy spray, her own pictures never looked right. She tried blue and green, red and violet, but something was always missing.

Her drawing was not the ocean.

Goldie kept trying, until her favourite pink crayon broke in two. Foss was sympathetic, but Jake just laughed. "That was the wrong colour anyway," he said. "Why don't you just go and see the ocean for yourself?"

"Do you know the way, Jake?" asked Goldie.

"I can find it," boasted the parrot. "Why, I have the Seven Seas in me blood." But, secretly, he was not so sure.

So Goldie packed a chequered handkerchief
with three apples and a piece of cheese for herself,
some sunflower seeds for Jake, and a twist of
catnip for Foss. The three friends were ready.
Goldie tied the bundle to a stick and off they set.

They soon left their home far behind. Broad streets dwindled to narrow, winding lanes. The houses they passed grew older and the trees grew greener.

Before long they were travelling through bright yellow meadows and steep purple hills. When the sun went down they made a nest in the hayloft of an abandoned barn beside a river. Goldie and Jake curled up to sleep, but Foss prowled the night—to stand watch and keep them safe.

In the morning, they met a whistling boy who scuffled up from the riverbank. His eyes were black and bold and set in a soup-spoon face. "New here?" he asked. "Then come and see my boat!"

"Are we at the ocean?" asked Goldie.

"This is a river," said the boy.

He led them down to the river and onto the most beautiful boat that Goldie had ever seen.

"Not quite a pirate's vessel," sniffed Jake.

It was a canal boat, covered from stem to stern with paintings of roses and castles and curlicues.

"We're on our way to the sea," Goldie told the boy. "I have to see it before I can draw it properly."

"Why go to the sea?" answered the boy. "The ocean dwarfs everything. It makes the river look like a little blue birthday ribbon. Stay here. You can listen to the river rock you to sleep and never be alone. You can paint my boat instead of the ocean. You can be my family."

But Foss overheard and poked his head into Goldie's hand. "No, no," said Goldie, "we can't stay. We're off to seek the sea. Besides," she said, with a wink to Foss and Jake, "I already have a family."

So they said goodbye to the boy and decided to follow the river. But the stream twisted and turned and led them into a dark wood, where the water disappeared beneath a terrible tangle of brambles and roots. Goldie, Foss and Jake were lost.

"To the crow's nest," cried the parrot and flew to the top of a tree. "Methinks I see a light!"

Jake led his friends through a maze of trees until they reached a rickety little house.

An old woman sat on the porch, her bony lap aflood with cats. Cats were in the windows, cats were in the doors. Cats climbed on the roof and clung to the trellis. Cats scratched, cats licked, cats meowed, and cats slept.

"I don't like the look of this," muttered Jake. But Foss saw nothing wrong at all.

"Visitors!" cried the old lady. "Welcome! You are just in time for tea." And with that, she swept them, cats and all, inside.

After a cosy tea of hot biscuits and berry jam,
Foss made friends with the cats while Jake
perched in the rafters, alert, aloof, and feathers
ruffled. Goldie asked the cat lady how to get out of
the forest and where to find the ocean. "I want to
draw the sea," she explained.

"Ah, my dear," the cat lady answered at once,
"you'll not like it there. The ocean hisses like a
million angry cats. It eats up boats and sea
captains.

"And as for you," she said, turning to Foss,
"your paws will get wet and sandy, and your fur
will smell of salt.

"Stay with me," she said to Goldie. "I could
use a keen young helper here. You will be safe and
you can draw the forest."

It was warm and light inside the cottage. But
Goldie shivered when she saw the shadowy trees
outside the window. The sea felt far away.

Jake flew down to her shoulder. "Courage," he
whispered.

"Thank you just the same," said Goldie to the
cat lady, "but we must go on. My friends will help
me to be brave."

Goldie and Foss slept that night in a hollow log, while Jake kept the watch.

On the morning of the third day, on a little road through the woods, they met a grizzled old man driving a horse and cart. He doffed his cap and offered them a ride.

"Are you a gypsy?" asked Goldie. The friends climbed aboard the wagon, which overflowed with all manner of odd junk: pots and pans and puppets, old hats and feather dusters, wooden boxes and weather-vanes.

"Heavens, no," said the man. "It's a higgler I'm called—a peddler, a buyer and seller, a trader. I can sell you anything: a packet of pins, a fishhook, a lace collar or a pot of paint! Why, I make my own colours—oyster pearl, sand-dollar grey, anemone crimson. Heard of them?"

"Those are ocean colours!" cried Goldie.

"Oh, so you know the ocean, then?" asked the higgler.

"Not yet," said Goldie, "but it is my greatest wish to go there."

"I have been known to trade in wishes and dreams," the higgler said. "I might just give you a ride to the ocean if you give me a good reason why."

"Because I want to draw the sea," replied Goldie, "and I can't—not until I've seen it for myself." And then she told him the tale of her journey.

"Your wish," said the old man, "is granted!"

And so they travelled many miles until they reached the great cliffs where the land falls away to the sea.

Goldie danced for joy.

The higgler led them to the water's edge. Foss pawed at scarlet starfish, spongy seaweed and scuttling crabs. Jake and the higgler wandered down the long beach, poking at curved and spiky driftwood. They searched for buried treasure and colours for the paint pots.

But Goldie sat all by herself and gazed at her heart's desire.

She saw great waves rise and fall, fierce as lions against the rocks, but gentle as kittens when they lapped at the shore. She saw seagulls soaring high and smelled the sharp salt air.

She watched sea and sky touch each other so far away she couldn't tell which was which. And she studied the thousands of colours that played upon the water.

Goldie stayed and looked until the moon rose. There is so much to remember, she thought. Then Foss, Jake and the higgler returned.

"Take this," said the old man, placing a spiral sea shell in her hand. "Whenever you want to remember the sea, just close your eyes and hold this to your ear."

Goldie did, and heard great waves beating like a heart inside the shell. "It's time to go now," she said.

The higgler drove Goldie, Foss and Jake back
to their starlit street. When they had climbed
down, he reached deep into his cart and pulled out
three pots of paint—oyster pearl, sand-dollar grey,
anemone crimson—and gave them to Goldie.

"Goodbye!" she called to the old man. The
three tired friends walked on in silence until they
came to their little hushed house. They stepped
quietly over the threshold. It was good to be home.

The next morning, Goldie again ate her breakfast of porridge. After the bowls were washed, she fetched her crayons and coloured pencils and opened the higgler's pots of paint. Once more she held the sea shell to her ear.

Then Goldie began to paint the sea.

Jake flew down to her shoulder and Foss curled up in her lap. Together they watched as a magical picture flowed from Goldie's hands.

Deep within his throat, Foss began to purr.

For Bill, Alex and Raffi
J.S.

For Pam
K.L.

Text copyright © 1987 by Judith Saltman
Illustrations copyright © 1987 by Kim LaFave
First paperback printing 1991

Canadian Cataloguing in Publication Data

Saltman, Judith
  Goldie and the sea

A Meadow mouse paperback.
ISBN 0-88899-133-9

I. LaFave, Kim.   II. Title.

PS8587.A57G64 1991 jC813'.54 C90-095773-5
PZ7.S34Go 1990

Design by Michael Solomon
Printed and bound in Hong Kong
by Everbest Printing Co., Ltd.